After Here

After Here

Dave Wolffe

Charleston, SC
www.PalmettoPublishing.com

After Here

Copyright © 2022 by Dave Wolffe

First Edition

Hardcover ISBN: 979-8-8229-0675-4
Paperback ISBN: 979-8-8229-0676-1
eBook ISBN: 979-8-8229-0677-8

To my life partner, detail manager, and great supporter,
Betty Litto, and my loving family.

The rain was coming down more slowly now, turning into a fine, gentle mist. Joe Golden had been on the road for almost three hours. He was looking forward to getting home and climbing into bed. He was about twenty miles from home, on the familiar Route 9, going about fifty miles per hour. He felt his eyes beginning to close. In what was ten seconds, Joe's head jerked upward and his eyes opened wide as the loud horn blaring and the bright lights of a truck blinded him. During the next minute or so, there was the screeching of brakes, the crunching of metal, and the smashing of glass. The next things Joe experienced were a bright white light and the deafening sound of absolute silence. He would never again feel the covers he so desperately wanted to pull tightly around himself. Joe was about to take a new and certainly different journey.

Joe found himself gently being pulled upward, almost as if he was riding on an escalator, passing through soft, fluffy clouds with a gentle, warm breeze brushing against his face. It didn't take long for him to realize he had left the life he knew behind, including his two grown children, Carl and Ann, and his two grandchildren, Bobby, age six, and little Carrie, age two. He had also left the friends who he had traveled and done just about everything with and his career as an architect, during which he had developed his own successful business.

His wife, Arlyne, had come this way before him, succumbing to a three-year battle with cancer just a little over one year ago. He felt tears running down his cheeks. However, he was never one to dwell on anything, either good or bad. He wondered if you got to meet the people who had traveled this road before and if they would be greeting you when you arrived. Would his grandparents, Alan and Rita Golden; his dad, Robert; mom, Carol; maybe his friend Pete—who, like him, had come here after a car accident—be waiting to greet him?

A smile came over his face as the image of his wife appeared in his mind. "Will she meet me when I arrive? If not, how will I find her? What is life here going to be like? Will I be able to look after, guide, somehow protect Carl and Ann and Bobby and Carrie?" Questions, more questions, and still more questions went through Joe's mind. Before he had much more of a chance to think, Joe found the first part of his journey had ended.

Before him stood four divergent paths, each leading to a different neighborhood. The first road was bound on both sides by thick, shady trees, with their multicolored leaves beginning to fall. It continued as far as the eye could see. The next had snowcapped mountains of different heights on both sides. The third was lined with dunes of fine sand being gently blown around. The last path wound and zigzagged, going far into the distance. It had lush green grass and budding flowers.

Joe had to decide which road to travel on first. He knew he would want to explore them all. Time was no longer a limitation for him, a thought that brought a slight smile to his face. He certainly enjoyed the forest with its trees, birds, and brisk air, all of which he associated with his favorite season, fall. It also turned out to be the time of the year he made this trip.

Then there was the road through the sand dunes. Oh, how Arlyne had loved the beach, along with the warmth of summer. How she had looked forward to this season and all that it brought, including family vacations and barbeques. He could almost hear Bobby and Carrie laughing as they ate their hot dogs with mustard all over their faces. He could see Ann running after Carrie with a napkin and Kate trying to make her son sit down long enough to wipe his face. Then there was Carl, with his trusty camcorder, trying to get it all on film, as his son-in-law, Tom, ran in and out of the house trying to see how his amazing Mets were doing. Of course, there was Arlyne with her warm smile, taking it all in, as Joe worked hard to make the food just right. Oh, what a picture! It was something Joe and Arlyne would no longer be part of.

"Would Arlyne have chosen this road? If she did, how far did she take it? Could she still be somewhere along this road? How far do I have to take it to find out whether or not she's still on it?" A barrage of questions pounded through Joe's head. It was also the season she had died. Would this be a reason she wouldn't have chosen it? It was some time after his arrival, and still no welcoming committee or receiving line. The thought of being totally alone and the questions "For how long? And why?" went through Joe's mind. As he shook his head, the image of the TV show *Star Trek* with its crew landing on what seemed like a totally deserted planet appeared. Joe didn't spend much time thinking about how bad this could be.

He was a problem solver. His first job was to figure out how to begin adjusting to his new environment. This was not the first time he had to deal with new surroundings. There was college (three hundred miles away from home), the apartment he shared with friends, the first place he and Arlyne lived when they were first married, and finally, the house they bought once Carl and Ann came along. All of these moves were initially met by checking out the neighborhood. Joe was back to his original question of which road to travel first. Perhaps, as had been the case during these other changes, he would meet people and get more information on life in these new surroundings. Joe shook his head from side to side as he thought, "This is a totally different kind of neighborhood."

Before he had much more of a chance to think, Joe heard a rustling of leaves and the sound of something running in his direction. As he focused his attention on the path in front of him, he saw a black dog running toward him, vigorously wagging his tail. When he looked more closely, he noticed it was a Labrador retriever. All at once the dog was by his side, nuzzling against his leg. Joe bent down, scratched behind the dog's ears, and patted his head. The dog looked up at Joe.

Suddenly the man blurted out, "BARNEY!" The dog's tail wagged so hard that his whole rear end shook. Barney was the family dog that had been killed by a car two years before. Joe took Barney around his body and hugged and kissed him. The dog reciprocated by licking his owner's face repeatedly. This was Joe's welcoming committee. He no longer would be alone.

Barney had come down the path that was surrounded by huge shady trees. Joe decided this would be the road he would take. To the best of his memory, Barney's trip to After Here had been taken sometime during the winter. "This might explain why Barney was on this path and not the one that led through the snow-capped mountains. Maybe, just maybe, he came to bring me to Arlyne," he said to himself. He paused, then added, "My own direct messenger. How Arlyne loved Barney. For that matter, we all did, even Bobby." With that thought, more memories came to Joe's mind. "Barney let Bobby yank his tail, play with his ears, and even give him big hugs. He was such a gentle dog, full of love, a great companion. Whenever any of us were sad, Barn instinctively knew and would come over, put his head near us, or on our lap, and we'd scratch it and hug him. He was with us for eight years. We got him when he was a pup."

Joe looked down at Barney with a broad smile and started walking. The dog walked beside Joe, with his big, wide head looking forward and his tail wagging. His assignment was done. He had found Joe. Where they would end up was anyone's guess. Barney wasn't leading his owner anywhere, something that was disappointing Joe. He had hoped his faithful dog would take him to someone they both loved so much. He was frustrated. He thought that what really might have happened was that Barney got lost, wandered, and found him—not as he had truly wanted to believe, been sent on purpose.

As Joe and Barney started down the tree-lined path, a gentle, brisk flow of air reached them. It was the kind that heightens the spirit and helps to quicken the pace. Added to this sensation was the sound of birds sweetly speaking to each other. Joe looked at Barney, smiled, and petted his dog's soft head. How far would they travel? What or who, beyond nature's gifts, would they find as they continued on this journey? How long would exploring this part of Joe's new neighborhood take? For sure Joe had an abundance of questions about life in After Here. One thing Joe knew for certain; he would not be going back to where he started.

As Joe and Barney moved farther along the path, more multicolored leaves fell in front of them, and the sun directed its rays over more of their bodies. It seemed as if they were moving from the outskirts of this new neighborhood into a part of it where they seemed more welcome, at least by the natural environment. Barney left Joe's side, chasing a little gray squirrel that ran up a tree. He then scampered after some birds, who landed for a brief time before heading back to the clear blue yonder, where they would be safe from the dog's playful paws.

As he played, Barney barked, looking up with his soft brown eyes as each of the small animals went higher than he could reach. It was as if he was saying, "I want to keep playing!" and then asking, "What are you doing? Why are you leaving me?"

Joe was amused by his dog's antics, shaking his head from side to side and smiling. The thought of encountering another human being entered his mind. As it did, his smile disappeared, and his sparkling eyes turned into a blank stare.

As he walked, he realized how soft the ground felt. The dirt was free of rocks, and the gravel felt like a soft brown carpet. His mind returned to the apparent absence of humanity. As it did, he and Barney resumed their journey. All at once, the Lab started to bark again. This time he ran ahead, disappearing from sight. His barks continued, although sounding softer as he traveled farther away from Joe. Joe's pace quickened. He didn't want to lose his only companion. The dog's barks grew fainter. Joe began to panic. He was now running.

All of a sudden, he caught sight of Barney, whose tail was wagging so hard that his rear end moved with it. There, standing around taking turns petting him, were five people, all dressed in uniforms. Two were firefighters, two were policemen, and one was a female EMT worker. In the background was a group of men dressed in suits with ties and jackets. Standing around near them were women dressed in business outfits. Joe rubbed his eyes in disbelief. When these people remained in view, a large grin came across his face.

Before he had a chance to speak, the larger firefighter came over to Joe with his hand extended. "Were you there when the first or second plane hit the Twin Towers?"

It took Joe a brief minute to realize what this person was talking about. "No, I just arrived here. It's been twenty-one years since that horrible tragedy occurred. I came here as a result of a car accident." Without waiting for any further questions, Joe explained, "I fell asleep for a split second and awoke in time to see the large lights of a truck and hear its horn blaring. That was the last thing I remember."

Joe shook hands with John Connelly, who revealed that he'd been a firefighter for just two years. John introduced Joe to the other uniformed people and then to the other victims, who he'd discovered were on the top floors in the tower where the second plane hit. Joe wanted to ask so many questions about life in this neighborhood, but knew each of these people wanted to talk about their experiences on September 11, 2001.

He heard many details of the events that took place on that fateful day. Joe was able to view the scenes through the eyes of those who had actually been there. He had only seen pictures on television and read articles about the horror that took place, but could not truly understand what it was like for those who experienced it. With these personal accounts, he could actually feel the pain, the horror, the trauma of what these folks had gone through. He hadn't known anyone who was actually there. It became so real to him, he felt tears running down his cheeks. Joe could not help feeling shaken. He now had heard the accounts of five of the heroes who had made the ultimate sacrifice, giving their lives in the line of duty, along with some of those who were the civilian victims of that day's tragedy.

Joe felt his story was so insignificant compared to those who just had shared these emotional personal experiences. He wanted to say, "I'm here. It really doesn't matter what brought me" when he was asked to tell how he had arrived in this neighborhood. However, he felt that these people were willing to share their reasons for being in this place and they deserved, at the very least, his response to this question. It was also something Joe felt might establish a bond with them. For a while, Joe engaged some of these people in conversations about families and careers. There was no small talk about the weather or health, or for that matter, any gossip. For him, these were all time wasters, even though here and now there was plenty of time. Joe relished the opportunity of getting to know what was important to other people and felt he wanted to share his values as well. Getting to know them might determine whether or not Joe would want to return here after he found Arlyne.

Lisa Gonzalez, the EMT whom he'd met earlier, came over to him. Her words "I'm sure you must have a lot of questions about life here; I know I did," penetrated Joe's thoughts, almost bringing his mind and senses to full attention. He entertained another brief thought. "Arlyne could not only tell I wanted something but what it was as well. Was it female intuition or just a gift some people have, most of whom seem to be female?" Whatever the case, he certainly wanted to know more. At this point, Joe moved his head up and down.

Lisa smiled. She was pretty and someone he judged to be about thirty. "What do you want to know?"

Joe stared at Lisa, smiled, and explained. "I want to find my wife, Arlyne, who died a year ago. How do I do that?"

The young EMT worker scratched her chin. Her expression became solemn. "I really am sorry. I don't know. I haven't thought about looking for anyone myself." Before he had a chance to ask his next question, Lisa answered it. "We happened to come across each other totally by accident. As you are aware, we arrived here about the same time. I liked the woods and falling leaves and followed this trail. I happened to find the others as they were walking along this path. As it turned out, they reached here shortly before me. We've pretty much remained here since. We feel comfortable with each other and these surroundings."

It was at this point that Joe began asking a barrage of questions. "How do you spend your time here? Does it get dark? What do you do about food? About sleep? About changing temperature?"

Lisa smiled again. In a soft voice she asked Joe to think about where he was and then said, "This is a place where we have full-time comfort. We don't have the same needs as before."

Joe asked, "What's a day like for you, or is it one continuous day?" He was like an inquisitive three-year-old child, firing questions without waiting for the answers.

The words "Whoa, Joe, one answer at a time" brought Joe's attention away from Lisa and toward Travis Brown. He was one of the two police officers in the group who was approaching them. His partner, Lou Riker, also came over along with Sam Collins, the other firefighter. It was as if this group had been summoned to perform the service of acquainting a citizen with his new neighborhood.

Sam Collins, the oldest of the group, took the lead. "You see, Joe, what we do is determined by who we are and not what we were. We certainly won't be responding to any more alarms, since there are no fires here. Lou and Travis won't be chasing any criminals, since there is no crime. Lisa won't be attending to any sick or injured people, since everyone here is free of illness and safe from harm. The folks from the different companies and businesses won't be doing any business or making any money, since nothing is needed. This neighborhood was developed by the common bond which brought us here. You and any others who reach us are welcome to visit and speak with us, but can't stay here permanently. Our existence is determined by our need to watch over those who we left behind—our families, close friends, and colleagues—and to greet and welcome them when it is their time to arrive. You have to find those whose lives you shared, join them, and watch over those who are still living. How you do this is for you to discover, perhaps by chance or by finding a common thread that would bind you together."

As Sam was speaking, Barney came over to Joe and sat down, rubbing against his master's leg. All at once, there was a sudden breeze, and Sam and all those who had just been with them disappeared. The trees and leaves surrounded Joe and Barney, and the path appeared in front of them again. Joe was abandoned once more. He was free from the presence of other human beings but still had the company of his faithful traveling companion. Whether they would continue down this path, or find another, remained a mystery. Joe shook his head. "At least I know people are brought together by some common thread," went through his mind. "Barney, my faithful pal, we only have to figure out what group we belong to and then how we are going to find it. This could take quite a while, but we both have all the time to do it."

Joe was determined to solve this mystery to be with his Arlyne once again. How he would do this, no one could know. As quickly as this thought went through his mind, he called to Barney, as both continued along the path to who knew where. To find a common thread was one thing, to locate particular people was another. "These people we came across were there, and Barney found them. Is he the key to finding Arlyne?" As this question went through his mind, another quickly followed. "Is she part of a group made up of just family members or part of another that was developed for cancer victims, or perhaps some other group?" He would be able to answer these questions once he found his wife. This was his only singular mission now. Once he found Arlyne, they would be with each other for all eternity, just as they had pledged that they would when they were married in 1970. Joe realized it could be quite some time before he found his wife. He always was a patient person.

Barney and Joe continued on the path through the woods. The black Lab went off after some small animals. Joe took in the panorama of the burnt red, glowing orange, and shiny yellow colors of the leaves falling from their huge trees along the path that he and his dog were traveling. He felt the brisk gentle breeze against his skin. *"Oh, what a feeling!"* flowed through his mind as a broad smile developed on his face. His feet felt almost as if they could leave the ground, allowing Joe to float along the trail. Barney's short, playful barks brought his companion's attention out of this soothing and energizing scene. The dog came over to Joe, sat down, pointed his jaw upward, and waited for his friend to scratch his ear and pet his head. After this short bonding experience, Joe and Barney moved farther down the road.

All at once, the breeze came to a complete halt, the leaves stopped falling, and the sounds of the creatures in this forest suddenly ceased. All signs of life came to a screeching halt. Joe's eyes widened, and his heart began pounding loudly. Barney's tail started wagging feverishly, and a smile almost seemed to appear on his face. Joe looked at his companion and realized that Barney knew something he didn't, and it wasn't bad. Both man and dog waited. There was a soft whooshing sound, like the surf rolling in toward the beach. An arch of soft colors formed beneath a fluffy white cloud, which descended onto a clearing just a few yards to the right of the path on which they were standing. The image of a man wearing a white suit with a light blue pastel tie appeared. He had snowy white hair and a gentle smile and stood about six feet tall. Joe rubbed his eyes. Barney ran over to the man, sat down, and looked up at him. He could have been a new arrival to this neighborhood, or someone famous, judging by his entrance, or…

As Joe tried to figure out the answer to the question of this being's identity, the person spoke. "Hi, Joe. Welcome to your new home!" Joe smiled, as the man, or whoever he was, continued. "I'm sure you have many questions."

"That's an understatement," Joe silently responded.

This unknown person spoke once more. "I am your guardian for the rest of eternity. There are no careers to follow, no money is needed, and your comfort is always provided. Knowing what I already know about you, your first major undertaking is finding Arlyne." Joe's mouth dropped wide open. "No, Joe, I won't tell you where she is or what you need to do to reach her. You may be angry with me for not helping you, but things occur when you make them happen. You create your own life, your own fulfillment." Anticipating Joe's next question, he said, "What I do is make sure you are comfortable and keep an eye on the people left behind. You will feel my presence as you move further down this road, or any other paths you choose to follow.

Joe stared at the image of this being, whose existence he had questioned. Before he was able to describe his feeling, the Guardian disappeared. "Man, who needs a *presence*. I need answers to questions that *he* doesn't want to answer for me. What good is *he!*" He punctuated this thought by shaking his head. Joe was determined to find Arlyne, without the assistance of even the most powerful source imaginable.

As Joe and Barney continued on their journey, a ray of light pierced through the trees, pointing downward. As it penetrated the layers of clouds, it circled as a plane might as it approached an airport. It seemed to be searching for something or someone. A scene materialized. It was a cemetery. The beam of light moved closer. There were many people gathered around one particular gravesite. A man holding a prayer book and wearing a yarmulke (skullcap) was speaking. Four adults stood closest to him and to the open grave. Two young children, holding their mother's hand, were standing there as well. Standing on the opposite side were two men. One was holding a shovel, scooped a small amount of dirt, and threw it into the open grave, while the other waited to repeat this ritual.

Joe started to cry. It was his family. It was his funeral. It signaled an ending to his life on earth for those he left behind. As soon as he made this connection, the beam of light retracted back into the sky. As it was withdrawn, it rose above the clouds, back through the path, which was sealed again. Joe shook his head. "Why now?" Perhaps it was the Guardian, providing Joe with the opportunity to see the people he had left behind. Just as Joe's mind ended this train of thought, Barney came over to his friend, sat down, and looked up. In an instant, he found his head being stroked and Joe's arms surrounding his body, hugging him. Barney wagged his tail, and made what sounded like a purring sound.

It wasn't too long before man and his best friend were on their way again. As they walked along the path, Barney's ears went up, and Joe began shaking his head in disbelief. The sound of a guitar playing and a male voice singing became louder. As Joe looked away from the path, he saw a wooden stage with a small group of people standing and clapping their hands as the performer sang. Joe and Barney watched and listened for a few minutes to the lyrics: "Country roads, take me home, to the place I belong." Joe knew who it was. He couldn't help smiling as he turned back on the path. Barney followed along right behind Joe.

"How about that, Barn, a live"—he smiled—"John Denver concert, right here in our new neighborhood." They walked for a while. Joe was humming the melody to the song, and Barney seemed to skip along behind him. Joe had wanted a diversion, and he'd gotten it—a glimpse of the people he left behind and a concert. Maybe part of the power of living in this neighborhood was just to think of something that you wanted and you got it. "Wow! What a concept!" he thought. A big smile appeared on his face. He would put this idea to a test.

Joe and Barney continued on the path. Their pace was steady and brisk. The dog scampered off and barked a few times. Joe's thoughts were focused on finding Arlyne. There was a vigorous breeze now blowing. It seemed to get stronger as they moved forward. Joe thought this shouldn't be happening in this climate-controlled neighborhood. He decided to go off the path, away from the wind, and explore more of the forest. He knew he wouldn't go too far because he wanted to return to the road once the wind subsided. This was something he hoped wouldn't take too long.

Barney looked up at Joe. His gaze seemed to question this new direction. Joe looked down and sensing his dog's concern said, "Barn, we're just going a little way. We'll see what great things we can find away from our path; then we'll go back on it again. Okay, ole boy?" As he finished this explanation, he patted his companion's head. Barney now trotted alongside Joe. They walked ahead, going about half a mile into the woods. The trees were larger than those found along the path, with a great deal of multicolored leaves falling. A ray of light shining straight down seemed to illuminate the new trail Joe and Barney were now following. Blue jays and robins flew between the trees ahead of the man and dog, seemingly trying to catch a glimpse of the two newcomers. Squirrels chattered on branches and scurried up and down tree trunks. Joe looked at Barney. "Seems like they're looking us over and trying to figure out why we're here." The dog looked up, then straight ahead.

They went about ten yards farther before they reached a clearing. There was nothing and no one around. It was a small space, about the size of a large area rug. As they approached this clearing, Joe heard the rustling of branches beyond it. Barney started barking loudly. Four people, two couples, one older than the other, became visible as they came closer to Joe and Barney. As they continued toward this group of people, their faces became clearer. They recognized Joe, and he knew who they were.

"Mom, Dad, Grandma, Grandpa" came flying out of his mouth. He kissed his grandmother and grandfather and hugged them tightly. His dad came over with arms extended. Joe ran into them in the same way you might expect to see a young child do with his father who had been away for a long time. He went over to his mom, held her tightly, and gently kissed her cheek. No sooner did this display of affection end than Joe looked past his parents and grandparents toward the opening where they had entered the clearing. His stare was intense and prolonged. Barney moved past Joe's family, got some pats on the head, and sat beside his master. He, too, looked toward this part of the forest.

Joe realized it wouldn't be at this place or at this time that Arlyne would join him. If she were here, she would have been with the rest of his family. Joe's grandmother, Rita Golden, put her hand gently on her grandson's shoulder. Her husband, Alan, stood beside her. Joe's mom and dad joined them. Robert Golden's face reflected his son's disappointment. "We've been watching you since we left. We are so proud of you. We wish we could have been there to see Carl and Annie graduate from college, get married to Katie and Tom, and see our grandchildren, Bobby and Carrie. It would have been so special for us, and mom and dad, to be part of all of your lives."

Joe looked up at his dad, shook his head, and quietly said, "We all missed out."

Carol Golden smiled at her son and softly uttered, "Watching from a distance is a small consolation."

Joe's mom then took the conversation in another direction. "We really felt badly for you when Arlyne joined us here." As if anticipating her son's reaction, she continued. "We were all able to greet her when she arrived. We had plenty of time to get ready, and thanks to the Guardian, knew where and when she would be entering our new world."

Carol Golden knew her son well and stopped just long enough to catch her breath. "When Arlyne came, she was scared and angry. She couldn't bear to leave you and the kids. She was most upset about being without you and how you would deal with her absence." She paused again. "The Guardian let Arlyne keep an eye on you until she saw you adjust and go on with your life. When you were working again, building your business, seeing the kids and grandkids, and involved with your friends again, she knew you would be okay."

Before Joe could ask why she wasn't with his parents and grand-parents, his mom continued. "Arlyne told us she wanted to find her sister and parents. She knew about the four paths and asked us if we saw any of them. We did see her mom and dad. They had come to the entryway to the paths to wait for their other daughter, Diane." She paused for a second, shook her head, and added, "What a tragedy to see both children die at such young ages and leave behind husbands and children." Joe's mom knew her son wanted to hear more about his wife. "Anyway, we came to welcome John Daly, one of your dad's closest friends from college."

Joe nodded.

Robert Golden jumped into the conversation. "John had a heart ailment, which necessitated taking him through many operations, much pain, and finally, after two years, he lost his battle with his illness."

Joe stared at his mom, who clearly knew her son didn't want to hear any more details about John Daly. "We told Arlyne we saw her parents go down the Path of the Dunes." She smiled, then added, "They enjoyed the beach and warm weather as much as she did."

Joe's eyes gave his mother a definite message for the second time.

"Arlyne went down that path, and that was the last time we saw or heard from her." Carol Golden anticipated her son's next question. "There is no way to know how far or how long you travel here. We all have plenty of time to do whatever we choose to do, whenever we choose to do it."

Joe sighed. He didn't bother to ask questions about how his parents and grandparents dealt with these surroundings and the world of After Here.

As Joe was about to speak, Robert Golden anticipated what he knew his son was wondering, and responded. "We've been told somewhere along the Path of the Woods that you were on, there is a turnoff that may lead you to the Path of the Dunes. We don't know how far it is or how long it will take, but one traveler said he saw it somewhere in the direction you were going." Joe's eyes widened. His dad continued. "Or, you can retrace your journey to the junction where all the paths meet."

Joe decided he would continue on the path he and Barney were taking. "Dad, we'll continue." He took a deep breath. "I think when we can find the turnoff," he said, hoping it was indeed there, "we will be on our way to the Path of the Dunes and closer to where Arlyne is."

All at once Carol Golden spoke. "Stay here awhile. We haven't seen you for over ten years, and your grandparents for even longer. We want to tell you so much. We miss talking with you."

Before her words had a chance to settle in Joe's ears, he responded, "Not now, Mom. I'll get back sometime. I've got to find Arlyne." With those words spoken, he called Barney and started walking back to the trail from which they had wandered.

Joe's mom turned to her husband, shaking her head from side to side, and said, "Some things never change." Robert Golden smiled.

Alan and Rita Golden waved to their grandson, who was going to continue his quest. Who knew how many roads he would have to try or how far he'd have to travel to find his wife. Joe was sure of two things: he had all the time he needed and would definitely find Arlyne.

Joe and Barney moved farther down the Path of the Woods. The black Lab was doing his thing. His human companion went along, watching the leaves falling, listening to the sounds of the animals, and feeling the brisk soft breeze, all of which contributed to experiencing this environment. On and on this twosome traveled. Joe hoped he would soon find the road that would lead him to the Path of the Dunes and maybe to his beloved Arlyne. They had gone about a mile when Joe looked up and saw and heard something that didn't blend with the large shady trees shedding their colorful leaves. He heard screeching sounds and saw gray-and-white seagulls with curved beaks flying above. As he watched them circle, he noticed a ray of light shining toward the ground. It shone on a clearing just about one hundred feet from the path Joe and Barney were taking. He saw a path beyond the clearing and watched as the seagulls headed in that direction. He called to Barney and said, "Looks like we found the turnoff! Let's follow that path and see where those birds are going." Joe crossed his fingers and looked up at the sky.

"Opportunity seems to be knocking at my door. Looks like our guardian is at work," Joe said as he looked down at Barney, whose eyes were fixed on him. They followed the gulls on the path they had found. Soon the trees began to thin out in number and size. As the man and dog continued on their journey, they came upon thin reeds of grass resting on small mounds of sand. Joe smiled. As he did, he petted Barney, whose tail began wagging enthusiastically. While they climbed over a few piles of fine white sand, they could hear the sound of water smacking against something hard and thunderous rumbles a distance away.

Soon they reached another sand dune that required more of their energy to climb. Joe needed to use both hands, as well as his feet, to get to the top of this small mountain. Barney pulled hard on all fours. They both finally reached the top of the mound and looked ahead. There was the water. "An ocean, or some reasonable facsimile of one," Joe thought.

As he looked harder, he could see a path. As Joe's eyes followed it, he noticed that it split into another going off into a direction away from the water. He saw this second trail went the way he and Barney had already traveled. It followed a line along smaller dunes with their reeds sticking upward. Both of these paths were hidden from each other. Joe had two decisions to make. The first, which road to travel. The second, whether or not he should go back and forth from one to the other, crossing the sand mountain so as not to take the chance of missing Arlyne. How would he figure out which was the Path of the Dunes that led from the entryway into the world of After Here?

As he stood thinking, seagulls circled above him, screeching loudly. Barney kept jumping up and barking at them. Joe had been "given" clues before. "Come on, Barney—let's stick close to the water for now. Arlyne loved the sound of the ocean. Maybe she followed it as she searched for her folks and sister."

As Joe walked along by the hardened sand, Barney ran around in circles, barking playfully and kicking up some of the finer particles of sand. Joe smiled and let out a big sigh. As the mellow voice of Nat King Cole singing the words "Those lazy, hazy, crazy days of summer" went through his mind, Joe found himself snapping his fingers and noticed a bounce come into his step.

Joe and Barney went along this path for about three more miles, enjoying the warm, silky sand underfoot and the comfort of the warm sunshine on their faces and bodies. All at once, Barney's ears went up like radar antennae, and Joe stopped right in his tracks. They heard the sound of objects hitting the water and a male voice shouting. Both noises came from just over the large sand dune that lay in front of them. Joe started to run toward the voice, with Barney running right beside him. When they climbed over this obstacle, they saw a person standing at the water's edge, his salt-and-pepper hair blowing in the breeze as he stared out toward the ocean. Joe looked in the same direction and knew why this person kept gazing toward the water. He, too, was taken in by the beauty of this scene.

As Barney and Joe moved toward the man, the dog barked. The man turned and started moving toward them with his right arm outstretched. The two men spontaneously smiled as they came closer to each other. "Hi, Joe," were the first words uttered by Pete, Joe's close friend. He had arrived less than a year before Joe, also as the result of a car accident. "I knew you were coming but didn't have enough time to get to the entryway to meet you." He paused, then continued. "I didn't know where you were after that and hoped we'd meet sooner rather than later."

Before Pete had a chance to say anything else, his friend asked, "Have you seen or heard anything about Arlyne?"

Pete's eyes widened, and a grin formed on his mouth. "I did see her. She stopped here for a while. She, like you, was really determined to find someone. In her case, Diane and her folks. I happened to have run into her sister, who was also looking for their parents. She told me they enjoyed the sand and water, but they also liked the lush green grass and bright budding flowers of spring as well. I see most of the people that travel along the Path of the Dunes, because here is where I spend my time."

He paused, then with another smile and his thumb pointed at his chest, said, "Consider me the beach ambassador. I told Diane and Arlyne I hadn't seen their parents pass here. Both sisters looked at me with their beautiful wide blue eyes and asked me how to find the Path of the Lush Green Grass and Budding Flowers. I only knew to go back to the entry point, which if I remember correctly, was some twenty-five or thirty miles back. I told them I did find out from others there are connector paths. None of these travelers knew exactly where they were. Diane and Arlyne decided to continue along this path. They hoped it would connect them to the path they wanted more quickly, rather than going back to the beginning of this road."

Pete quickly declared, "I want to stay here. It is what I dreamed this world would be like, and at the risk of sounding corny, it is heaven to me." He grinned and could see Joe was really impatient to continue his search.

"Pete, I want to spend more time with you, but that will have to wait. Right now, I need to find Arlyne." He shook hands with his college buddy and waved goodbye; then he and Barney left Pete to find yet another path. "Will I have to travel on all four paths before I find her? Will I have traveled far enough on any of these roads?" Both were questions he would not be able to answer until he completed his mission. Joe knew he would find Arlyne, but how far would he have to travel, and how much of his unlimited time would he have to use? These additional questions would remain unanswered until he reached his goal.

"I hope, Barney ole boy, the Guardian gives us another opportunity to find the Path of Lush Green Grass and Budding Flowers before we have traveled very far from here." Joe put both of his hands together to accentuate this thought.

Instead of chasing blue jays, robins, and squirrels, Barney went after seagulls. Joe walked along the path watching and listening to the surf coming and going and felt the gentle sea breeze brushing against his face, along with the soft, warm sand beneath his feet. He walked on, following the black Lab, who made it to the edge of the sand, barking and jumping as the sea birds escaped to the safety of the surf. They passed a reef, and then the sandy beach came to an abrupt halt. To the left of this point was a small sand dune with scruffy-looking reeds on it. Joe called Barney, who was oblivious to this change as he romped on the beach still barking at his new feathered playmates. His dog, finally realizing something was different, ran over to Joe's side.

Joe moved forward over the small hill. On the other side of it, about twenty feet ahead, was another path. This trail began by having small sandy hills, lined on both sides by sparse light-green blades of grass. This scenery continued for a few hundred yards. At this point, flower buds resting between thickening greener blades of grass replaced the less rich-looking vegetation. A smile appeared on Joe's face as he leaned down and petted Barney's soft head. "Finding this path so quickly could be a sign," he thought. "Hopefully, my search for Arlyne is almost over, if she's still on this path."

Joe and Barney continued farther along this trail. It led into another, which headed in the direction they had followed on the previous two paths. As they turned onto this road and continued along for a while, the grass became thicker and greener, and the buds changed into bright, beautifully colored flowers. Along with this picture came the sight of magnificently colored birds flying around meadows and the sounds of their sweet melodies. The farther along the Path of Lush Green Grass and Budding Flowers they traveled, the more beautiful this neighborhood became. The birds were singing their songs loudly as butterflies with bright-yellow wings and brown spots fluttered on both sides of the road. Barney scampered ahead barking at the birds and butterflies, running back and forth through the thick mint-green grass. He really seemed to be enjoying himself. Joe took in the aroma and sight of the beautiful rainbow colors of the flowers. For both man and dog, this seemed to be their favorite path so far.

As they walked farther along this road, they heard the sound of a horse neighing. Joe smiled. He and Arlyne had loved to ride horses together out in the countryside in Massachusetts. He could picture Arlyne's auburn hair, with streaks of gray running through it, flying in the wind and her cheeks turning a rosy red. As this memory ended, a beautiful chestnut horse appeared. Barney barked. The horse stared at him, pawing the ground with his right front hoof. He looked at Joe, who slowly walked up to this animal and stroked its neck. The horse didn't move. Joe then turned around, with this animal's long face resting on his shoulder and raised his arm, stroking the horse's face with his hand. "Could this be a messenger from the Guardian, Barney?" The dog looked up at him with a blank stare. "What could the message be?" Joe wondered.

All at once, the animal whinnied, gently pulled away, and ran off. Another thought occurred to him. "Arlyne's family owned a stable and had horses of their own." They had owned it until fifteen years ago, when her dad developed cancer. Ken Roth had been such a vibrant man before then. Once he contracted the disease, he became a frail old man. He died two years later, and was followed by his wife, Phyllis, three years after. They had enjoyed over forty-five years of marriage.

Diane, their other daughter, contracted the same disease and died two years after her mother.

As he thought about Diane's illness and death, Joe shook his head. "That was tragic. She was only forty-one and left behind two lovely little girls and her husband, Bill. Then again, my Arlyne was only forty-five." His face reflected the despair he felt.

It didn't take long for Joe to snap out of this mood as he yelled to Barney, "Let's get going, boy!" The dog ran to his companion's side, and they both moved forward again. It wasn't very long until Joe and Barney heard the distant neighing of a few horses and sounds of faint voices that were coming from the same direction. Joe's pace quickened. After they had gone a few hundred feet farther, the sounds became more distinct. Barney started barking loudly, his tail wagging wildly. As they went over a hill, they looked down. There they saw two women and a gray-haired man. Joe began waving and calling out. The three started moving their horses at a slow gait, and when they saw him more clearly, trotted toward him. Their faces became clearer. Joe couldn't help grinning widely.

As the younger of the two women saw him more clearly, her horse began to gallop. With her beautiful white teeth showing, she waved her arm and shouted, "Joe, it's really you!" Then, like a cowboy jumping off a moving horse running toward a local saloon for a most welcome drink, she ran right into Joe's outstretched arms.

At first, he thought it was Arlyne, because both sisters wore their auburn hair in ponytails and had similar builds. He then realized as she moved toward him who it was. "Diane," he called out, as they embraced and held each other for a few moments.

Just about the same time, Phyllis and Ken Roth came over to the two younger people and dismounted from their horses. Ken extended his hand, and Phyllis, in tears, went over to Joe and gently kissed him on the cheek. "Joe, we're sorry you came here so soon after Arlyne, but we are so glad to see you." Her face turned red from embarrassment, but Joe understood what she meant. He smiled and put his arm around his mother-in-law and held her tightly.

Joe looked at the horses and realized that the chestnut horse he had seen earlier was not among them. His expression showed the three Roths that something was puzzling him. Diane jumped in. "Joe, Arlyne was with us. She decided to ride a little further and stay out a little longer."

With his voice rising, Joe quickly asked, "Was she riding a beautiful chestnut horse?"

Ken responded. "Yes, she was riding Chief, the horse she owned and loved when she was in her late teens."

It occurred to Joe that the horse who had come over to him and Barney was Chief. He hadn't seen a rider. The horse didn't have a saddle. He remembered Arlyne loved to ride bareback. She'd always told him you could feel the strength of the horse, and really be with it in every way, if you rode it without a saddle. It wasn't something Joe could ever do. He was lucky to be able to ride at a trot, holding onto the horn of a western saddle without falling off. Whether he was good at it or not, he rode because his wife loved riding so much. He remembered Arlyne would ride bareback even with a horse she had ridden just a few times. Chief had been her horse. "No wonder he had no saddle," Joe concluded to himself. He thought some more. "I didn't see her when the horse ran off. She couldn't have been very far."

He was very excited. He smiled. Joe asked his in-laws how long they thought Arlyne would be until she returned.

"Joe, you know it could be hours. She loves to ride, sit somewhere and write poetry, then ride some more," Phyllis responded. "Your guess is as good as ours. You can be sure she'll be coming back—to *all* of us." She smiled, as did Joe.

His search was finally over. Now there was no need for Joe to travel on the Road of the Snow-capped Mountains of Different Heights. He and Arlyne could explore all the neighborhoods together like they had done when they were first married. They would also be able to watch over their children and grandchildren and maybe have some influence over their lives—surely not the way they could have if they were there. "Nothing is perfect, not even the Guardian's neighborhoods." Now it was just waiting—something he hated doing—but in this case, once it was over, he'd see his Arlyne.

"What will we say to each other? What will we do?" These were two questions he was anxious to answer. When they meet again, they would finally be able to honor their marital pledge: to be together for eternity.

Many readers like to have stories end in particular ways.
There are three possible endings.
YOU CHOOSE your own ending of After Here.

Ending #1

The Ambulance

All at once Joe heard voices. "He's coming around." Standing over him with stethoscopes hanging around their necks and wearing dark uniforms, two men looked down at him. As he felt a needle being put into his arm and heard the blaring of a siren, he realized he was inside an ambulance. Joe spoke, almost yelling, "OH NO!"

The two paramedics looked at him and had no idea why he had said that. They shook their heads from side to side and tried to calm him down.

Joe would have to wait to be reunited with Arlyne. This wasn't his time after all.

ENDING #2

Hospital Room

The voices were familiar to Joe. As he heard them, his eyes slowly began to open, and his eyelids fluttered, then slowly rose. He could see what looked like the foot of a bed, but it was unfamiliar. Slowly the haze lifted, and his vision began to clear. "He's getting up," the familiar female voice said. He heard loud movement and turned his head in its direction. "Dad, you're back from the dead," the male voice almost shouted. Little did he know.

Joe was puzzled. He began to speak, but his throat felt very dry.

"We'll get the doctor. She'll remove the tube they gave you to breathe better."

Joe shook his head horizontally, weakly at first, then more agitatedly. Carl held his father's arm, trying to comfort him. "Dad, it's probably frightening for you, and you must have so many questions. Wait until Dr. Ashek comes in with the nurse and they take out the tube."

Ann then leaned down and gently kissed her father's forehead. "Dad, everything is going to be all right."

Whatever had brought him back wasn't fair. He had been about to be reunited with Arlyne, his wife, his love, and now she was being taken away from him a second time. "Fair?" he thought. "Life—no, death—isn't fair!" As this idea went through his mind, tears trickled down his cheeks.

Carl and Ann both smiled. They thought their dad's tears were those of joy—at being alive, at being snatched from death's door.

"How could they possibly understand? They'd think I'm out of my mind if I told them about my experience visiting After Here."

ENDING #3

The Reunion

Arlyne turned Chief away from the path and pointed him toward the meadow at a gallop. Her hair, in a ponytail, bounced to the rhythm of her horse's gait. She'd been riding for a while. She stopped by a huge old oak tree, where she took out a writing pad. Her pen was poised as she waited for ideas to come. Arlyne was ready to absorb her impressions of the scene before her and put them into prose.

As she sat there, she dropped Chief's reins. He ran off at a trot, doing his own exploration of the surroundings. Arlyne glanced up only to see her horse heading over a hill that she knew led to the Path of the Lush Green Grass and Budding Flowers. This had become a routine with them. She knew her horse would come back to her as he always had.

As Chief disappeared from view, Arlyne focused her attention on the sights, sounds, and smells of spring's place in the world of the After Here. She became totally absorbed in the sweet fragrances of the grass and flowers and the fresh breeze gently sweeping along her face. Chief seemed to be taking longer than usual. "Something must have really captured his attention. Oh well, when he gets bored, he'll come back."

In the time it took Chief to return to Arlyne, she had completed two verses of a poem. "Not bad," she thought as she eyed her horse coming down from the top of the hill. When the horse reached her, he leaned his long snout down to her. She began to pet it and then stood up. As she stroked the side of his wet neck, she said, "I'm ready to go back to my family." She paused, then added, "If only Joe were there with Mom, Dad, and Diane." Arlyne knew her husband had reached the world of After Here, but because he had come so quickly, she hadn't gotten the chance to meet him at its entry point. Her parents and sister had told her to stay put, and Joe would eventually reach her. She knew for sure that he would.

As horse and rider neared the small group that anxiously awaited their arrival, Joe could see Arlyne's face. It looked as beautiful as ever. When Arlyne dismounted from Chief, not waiting for him to come to a complete halt, she, too, was beaming. She looked like the blushing bride who Joe remembered standing under a canopy with her veil removed from her face. How proud and happy he felt then, and how great he felt now. He ran over to her when she was about ten feet away. Arlyne almost leaped into Joe's arms. He held her tightly and swung her around and around. He put her down and reached for her hand. They looked at each other and almost in chorus exclaimed, "Never again will we be apart!" They could now make good on their promise to be with each other for all eternity.

About the Author

Dave Wolffe, MS, was an educator/guidance counselor in the New York City public school system for over 30 years. He was also an adjunct lecturer at John Jay College of Criminal Justice in its conflict resolution program. Dave is the author of *Peace: The Other Side of Anger,* which is used in an anger management program he developed for and with teens, and *Settling the Unsettling: Understanding and Resolving Conflict,* which is used with college students. He currently resides in Connecticut.

www.ingramcontent.com/pod-product-compliance
Lightning Source LLC
Chambersburg PA
CBHW060924130726
48001CB00006B/2402